DUHARE

LARRY POWELL

GOTHAM BOOKS

Gotham Books
30 N Gould St.
Ste. 20820, Sheridan, WY 82801
https://gothambooksinc.com/
Phone: 1 (307) 464-7800

© 2022 Dr. Larry Powell. All rights reserved.

No part of this book may be reproduced, stored in a retrieval system, or transmitted by any means without the written permission of the author.

Published by Gotham Books (June 15, 2022)

ISBN: 978-1-956349-84-9 (sc)
ISBN: 978-1-956349-85-6 (e)

Because of the dynamic nature of the Internet, any web addresses or links contained in this book may have changed since publication and may no longer be valid.

The views expressed in this work are solely those of the author and do not necessarily reflect the views of the publisher, and the publisher hereby disclaims any responsibility for them.

Table Of Contents

Prologue

Ahki, a member of the Moundbuilder culture, struggles to survive in a world beset with natural and human dangers. Comets and volcanoes have forced him to leave his Enchanted Valley of the Ohio and Scioto River basins. It's the Sixth Century A.D., and natural catastrophes have plunged his world into a nuclear winter. In order to survive, he and two companions are making their way south to hopefully a warmer climate. Along the way they encounter people who are also struggling to survive, and who decided that raiding and killing if necessary might be their only chance to survive.

CHAPTER 1
CAVE-IN-THE ROCK

Our journey south was interrupted by the place of my nightmares. The same place where I was once held captive again became a place where I would stare death in the face. The only difference was that this time I seemed to have a better chance escaping death or capture. The current was swift, and the raiders were nowhere near their canoes. Their only chance of slowing us down was to make a lucky shot with one of their arrows.

Kolman and Kyana were doing their best to paddle furiously away from the raiders. In the middle of our boat I did my best to return fire at the raiders to keep them from reaching our boat. Kolman and I would occasionally retreat near the bottom of the boat to avoid the swarm of arrows coming our way, but Kyana kept paddling knowing that the quicker we got to the swifter current, the sooner we could escape down river.

The first arrow that struck any of us was a glancing blow that struck Kyana in the right shoulder. I yelled at her to get down into the boat, but she only changed paddling sides. She did manage to duck down after each stroke, yet I think this might have been what caused her demise. The arrow struck her temple with such a glancing force that it knocked her out of the boat. I immediately stood up to dive inafter her, but Kolman struck me on the legs with his paddle, and told me to keep on paddling. He said she was gone. The raiders would not get her. The Great River took her for his own prize.

We had managed to head into the swiftest part of the river. Knowing the raiders might take to their boats; Kolman and I continued to paddle until we were at the point of total exhaustion. Our strokes became fewer and fewer until the only sound was the river herself. It seemed that we floated forever until the last rays of the sun were beginning to fall behind a ridge of trees in front of us. Neither one of us had spoken to the other after Kyana had disappeared into the muddy depths of the Great River. I told him that I spotted a sandbar and small creek ahead, and that we should stop here for the night. With only a grunt and a nod of approval, he helped me steer the boat toward our campsite.

This would turn out to be one of the longest nights for both of us. We both said prayers and lit fires for Kyana. He turned in before me, and I could hear the occasional prayer of tears. I too stayed awake with thoughts of Kyana. Her smile and laughter seemed to help me through these dark times of frightful weather and mercilous raiders. Would I ever again find a woman who could give me a reason to live. We spent the next morning in quiet reflection. I was able to catch a few fish, and prepared themover a small fire.

"Kolman, come and eat. Let us say a prayer for Kyana. Her bravery keeps us alive onthis journey."

"It is times like this Ahki that make me wonder about the Great Spirit. Is she so selfish thatshe wanted Kyana back. Was Kyana's purpose to save us from the raiders?"

"The Great Spirit has a plan for all of us. Is it luck or is it providence?"

After our meal we discussed the rest of our journey. We were close to one of the many rivers that madetheir way south. Kolman said that he thought that he knew most of the clans south of here. There would be no large settlements until we reached Fort Mountain. I was looking forward to making it that far. Kolman had told me stories of the clans that lived near the mountain. The most interesting one was the moon-eyed people. They lived underground, and ventured outside mostly at night. Their hair was white, and their eyes the color of the sky. He mentioned that the legend was that they had had built the large walls that covered the top of the mountain. .They were afraid of someone or something.

Our first series of rivers reminded me of the Deer River back home. They were slow moving, and were alive with creatures coming to the river for water. Most were familiar to me. On occasion we would seeblack bears with their cubs. I knew enough from stories that female black bears were ferocious when protecting their young. One story involved a girl in our clan who had ventured into a berry patch to pickthe black berries. She didn't realize that a bear and her cubs were already there. She startled the momma bear, and the bear saw her as a threat. They found her partially buried body near the patch.

None of the other animals seemed to pose any threat. Some of the larger cats that we were familiar with hunted mostly at night. A huge fire always seemed to protect us. At night we could hear the sounds of the smaller cats. They sounded like one of our young children. The big cats had an entirely different sound. Before we had left The Enchanted Valley we had reports of wolves coming into camp. The colder weather was driving us south, and it seemed to do the same thing with the wolves. Other night creatures included the smaller wild dogs who loved to howl at night.

We were fortunate to stay away from the dangerous four legged animals, and the even more dangerous two legged ones. In the only dangerous encounter were lucky to be rescued by some local hunters who actually had driven the monster toward our camp one early morning. We had packed up our things and were heading toward the boat, weapons in hand. Kolman had a spear in his hand, and maybe this gave him the courage to go after it. It was heading toward a small group of hills, and Kolman was in pursuit. It was larger than a dog, and any creature this size would provide us with meat for the trip. The problem with most animal hunts is the speed of the critter. Deer were always hard to chase down, and this black squatty creature ran quickly for an animal its size. The difference between this creature and others that we had hunted was that this one stopped. I was trying to find my bow, but was keeping an eye on Kolman and the beast. But this prey was different. He stopped and instead of heading up the hill, ran straight at surprised Kolman. He managed to stab the beast with his spear, but not before it struck Kolman in the leg. This animal had a larged curved tooth on each side that protruded from its mouth. Its flat nose gave it plenty of room to swing these teeth, teeth that were as sharp as a flint knife.

It seems the hunters were trying to wear this animal down, and Kolman's cries gave them the direction of their prey. They acted as if they had seen this kind of wound before. Kolmans leg was cut just above the ankle, almost to the knee. Thank goodness it was not a deep wound, and the hunters quickly stopped the bleeding with moss and some kind of rope made from either vine oranimal material.

After our new friends had saved Kolman's life for now, we all retired to a shade tree to catch our breath. After some quick introductions, the hunters went to gut the creature. I told them they could have the meat, but they said they would share it with us. They decided to cook the meat over an open fire, and to dry it out to where it would last for a few days. I had seen these creatures before, but had never hunted them or ate them before. The meat was salty to the taste, and the smoke from the fire made them a tasty meal indeed. This was the best meal of the trip so far, and we ate to the point of sickness.

The only other meal like this had been the feast of the snake. We had killed and eaten the snake with the rattles, just after we had made our way south from the Great River. It was in an area that was rather swampy, and we had first just killed the dangerous critter in self-defense. Kolman had asked me if I had ever eaten snake, and my response was that I had not. We had clan members that had died from the bite of these creatures, so our people simply tried to stay away from them. The most plentiful snake in the Enchanted Valley was the black snake, and we tried not to kill them as they ate rodents and other nasty creatures.

Kolman had dispatched the snake with his spear, and proceeded with a sharp flint knife to remove the skin, and as much bone as he could. The rattles he used for a necklace, and I told him any of our shamans would value these as prized possessions for any ritual or ceremony. He then made a fire, and used a forked stick that he put the meat on and placed near the fire. You could see the juices dripping from the snake like rain, and the aroma was such that we both almost burnt our mouth after removing it from the stick. The biggest problem I had with this food was after I ate it. We were so famished, and ate so fast, that we both became ill. Kolman said the meat was of a richness that would cause one to vomit if they ate too much. He was so right, and I think I lost most of the nourishment that I had ingested.

After the meal with the hunters, they packed up, and said that they were making their way back up north. They asked where we were going, and Kolman said our next stop for some rest would be at a place that he called Singing Shoals. The hunters were familiar with the place that they called the River That Sings. They said they had been there a few times for trade, and the abundance of fish in the area. We thanked them for their help as they made their way away from the river. We had enough meat to last until the Singing Shoals, and once there we were confident that we could catch enough fish for mostof our journey.

Chapter 2
Singing Shoals

For the next few sun cycles our journey was surprisingly uneventful. Early in our journey we had tired ofeating fish, and now we were tiring of eating meat from the beast with tusks. Kolman said that in the Singing River that we would find shellfish similar to the freshwater clams of Paint Creek. He described them as being in a much darker shell, and were somewhat smaller than the clams.

After a few more sun cycles we began to see more and more fisherman. Kolman knew that we were getting closer to settlements along this river. One such fisherman directed us to the hut of a local shaman called Unashay.

"Welcome my friends. I hear you are heading to the Great Sea."

Kolman told him the story of our journey, and when I spoke it was mostly to ask questions about the people who lived along this river.

"How did this river get the name Singing River?"

"The river is a woman my friend. When she is happy and the water is low she sings a happy song. When the water is high she sings an angry song. The many shoals and water falls along her create the sound almost of a woman's voice. You can hear these sounds from far away, and if we stop talking you can hear them now. Some people however tell the story of a woman that lives in these waters who is half fish and half woman."

We talked more about the river, and I asked more questions, especially about raiders, and to my relief he said that he had heard stories, but only from people from the north. I decided to ask more questions about the river, especially the half fish half woman stories.

The stories varied, as different warriors had heard different versions. One tale involved a warning to any maidens that might be tempted to swim in one dangerous part of the river. Two girls defied their mothers warning and went swimming in this dangerous spot. They swam so long that they turned into fish. Their bodies were slimy, and they swam in a slimy part of the river that would glow at night. After swimming in this slime their hair became blacker and their eyes were bigger and brighter. On their arms grew silvery bands of glowing seaweed.

The other story involved three young boys who were walking across the shoals part of the river that had some exposed rock. The rocks were also slippery and one of the boys slipped into a deeper part of the river. His parents went to the local shaman for prayers. The shaman said the boy was not dead and that they could see him if they came early at sunrise on the bank of the great river. Word spread and a great crowd gathered at the spot where the boy was lost. At sunrise a large whirlpool began to form and up from the depths came a beautiful humanlike woman with a great fishtail. In her arms she carried the alive young boy and swam him to the bank and his joyful parents.

We said our thank you and goodbye to Unashay. Our next stop would be at one of the villages along the river. It would be a place where we could pick up provisions for the next stop which Koman described as Fort Mountain. We made one more camp before the village and my dreams that night were strangely related to the singing river. In my dream the singing was not caused by the rocks or shoals in the river, but came from the beautiful maiden that was half human half fish. In my dream she swam to the bank and spoke to me of the future:

"Ahki, wake up. I am Nunnuhsae or spirit of the river. I will protect you as long as you stay close to me. Danger awaits you at Fort Mountain. If you survive the evil there you will complete your voyage to the Great Sea. As for this river the music will always continue. The humans that will live here in the future will come from all over. Their music will be preserved forever on pieces of round wood. Time for you to move on."

I awoke suddenly to remember those last words, albeit I had no idea what "round piece of wood" meant but I surmised it was a prediction for the future. My old body was slow to move, but I was anxious to move quickly to the village and to obtain what we needed to maintain our trip. I would occasionally think of the warning in my dream, but after all the danger I had been through I was no longer afraid.

The Shoals as I called it was basically a fishing village. Our plan was to stock up on supplies here and then move south where we would need to portage with our boat. Something we were getting more and more acquainted with. We would also soon be entering the mountains, and as Kolman pointed out, then we would enter a stretch of rivers that would lead us to the Great Sea.

These people, and the ones that we were to encounter later, were master fisherman. The series of rocks in this river formed natural fish traps. The locals enhanced the ability to catch fish by building traps that captured the fish as they swam over the rocks. They also built traps near the shallows that had small entrances that lead into a much larger basin. The fish found their way in through the small entrance, but had trouble finding their way through the small exit.

The other interesting way that they acquired game was through deception. I had heard of such hunting techniques, but had never seen it in action. It involved the making of figures out of wood that would look strikingly like the water birds that they were hunting. These floating replicas would draw in other like birds to what they thought was going to be a safe place. They would then use nets and clubs to dispatch the birds. I never saw this in action as it was a seasonal thing, but they did show me the artistry of the decoys down to a like color of the water birds.

Before we left we sat around the fire on the last night and retold some of the stories that we had heard on our venture, and especially the ones along this river. I asked about the people who lived in and around our next stop. It was a place called Fort Mountain where Kolman would get the supplies we needed for our final push toward the Great Sea. Those around the fire seemed scared to mention one clan who lived there called the moon eyed people. I wasn't sure what this meant, but I guessed that they had problems seeing during the day, and one traveler to that area said they had white skin. They seemed afraid to talk about them but I could sense that there was something about them that upset the people of the shoals.

Chapter 3
The Great Blue Hills Of God

The next day we headed down river with enough supplies to get us to the larger mountains to the south. These mountains would end up being the largest and most mysterious mountains that I would ever encounter. I had only known the small foothills of The Enchanted Valley. These were double and maybe triple the size of those little bumps.

We had to drag and carry our boat through many a small portage, but now we were faced with many days of dragging and carrying. Kolman had faced this problem a few times before. We both decided the best plan was to abandon the boat, and to possible try and obtain another boat when we got closer to the rivers that would take us to the big sea.

After a few days of heading toward the rising sun, we soon came upon the mountains of my dreams. They were enormous, and it seemed like we were getting closer, but the biggest ones seemed to remain in the distance. Our food supply of dried fish was dwindling, so we turned to the natural growing plants in the area. One I was familiar with. It grew on a short bush, and the natives called it the papaw. We had them in The Enchanted Valley, and I remember the fruit to be sweet and ripe to the point where it was almost rotten.

The night air here in the mountains had us looking for some kind of shelter that would provide us with a few degrees of warmth. I also discovered my love for a fruit that was unheard of in The Enchanted Valley. The sweet blue fruit had an easy name of blueberries. As luck would have it we found a nice patch of them near the entrance to a small cave. Kolman pointed out however that patches of fruit like these attracted bears and other dangerous creatures. I would find out that night what he meant by other.

Even though the cave offered us some protection, Kolman recommended that we construct a small palisade to protect us from snakes and the like. We placed our spears against the palisade and proceeded to make a small fire for warmth and added protection against critters. Our meals of the evening was what I called blueberry soup. It was tasty, but seemed to run through my body and point me in the direction of the nearest bush.

It was long after our meal that I began hearing the sounds. It sounded like whistling coming from one ridge and being answered by something on the opposite ridge. We also heard a thumping sound like someone was hitting itself on its chest. We had not seen a soul for days, and Kolman said there were no clan sites nearby.

On one of my trips to the local bush I discovered the source of some of the sounds. Some distance away I saw a hairy man. He was standing beside a pine tree, and when he saw me he ducked behind the tree and would poke his head out to take a look. Kolman must have seen it to as a spear stuck itself in the tree the creature was hiding behind. After that we saw the huge creature with brownish black hair running up the side of the mountain. We hoped this would have scared him and his clan away, but we were unfortunately mistaken.

From the top of a nearby ridge we could make out the sounds of at least two of the creatures engaged in what can only be described as some kind of communication. This alerted us to the chance that they would return so we continued to stoke the fire, and to make torches that could be thrown as a weapon if necessary. .We had spears and rocks that we could throw as projectiles. We had no desire to fight these creatures hand to hand.

It seems that we were not the only ones who considered using rocks as a weapon. Our first hint of an attack came from the sound of a rock striking a nearby tree, and the whooshing sound of a huge boulder fling over our heads. If the hairy men would have been accurate we probably wouldn't be telling this story. We stayed low behind our barricade the rest of the night.

Apparently the hairy men were tired of throwing projectiles as they moved closer to us, so close that we could see them perfectly. The most striking feature was its enormous size, about twice the size of the largest of our people. It was hairy and brown with apparently a small or no neck. The creature also had red glowing eyes. When it started beating on its chest we guessed that an attack was coming

Thank goodness only one of them attacked. We were able to slow him down by launching rocks and a few spears that struck the mark. The creature kept letting out eerie howls, but he kept on coming. It wasn't until we managed to hit him with a large torch that the attacked subsided. Part of his fur caught fire, and he squealed back up a nearby hill. We heard sounds all night but none of them returned. By sunrise all of the sounds had subsided.

The next morning we decided to leave camp and find a safer place where we could get some rest. All around our camp were giant footprints. They were twice the size of a normal person's foot. We also had the smell of burning hair and what could best be described as rotting food. The last sign of the hairy men was at the top of the ridge where we had first seen them. In a clear patch of dirt was a print that can only be described as a giant ass print. It seems the hairy men had been sitting and watching us.

We walked as far as we could to distance ourselves from the territory of the hairy men. After we passed what we considered a territorial sign, we felt confident that we could get a goodnights sleep. We had a good laugh about the giant ass print. I asked Kolman why he snuck up to the top of the ridge to spy on me. Our laughter was interrupted by lights in the sky. At first they looked like giant fireflies, but their movement was erratic and their color was like the inside of some of the sunflowers I picked. It surely interrupted our sleep, yet it lasted only a short time. I couldn't shake the idea that the hairy men had something to do with it.

The hills that I was accustomed to were now being replaced with mountains. Kolman said the locals called these mountains The Great Blue Hills of God. He also said that we would not encounter any major rivers until we got south of Fort Mountain. A village after Fort Mountain would be Etowah, and the river system next to it was rich in shellfish and other water creatures. The night before we reached Fort Mountain he spent sometime explaining why our stay at Fort Mountain could be short lived.

"There have been times Ahki that we have decided to stay less than a day at Fort Mountain. There is a tribe that lives near the top of the mountain that differ from those that inhabit the region. They call themselves Allegewi and the locals call them moon eyed people."

"Is this strange tribe the reasons for your short stay?"

"More or less. It seems sometimes the Allegewi will roll boulders down to attack anybody who might try to reach the top of the mountain. They are said to live in caves and are tall with light skin."

"They sound like the old ones that we drove out of the Enchanted Valley. They all weren't of giant size, but some, especially the leaders were enormous. I have heard stories that some of them were peaceful, and even intermarried with some of our people. Some of the leaders moved a group of warriors south of the Great River, and I think these were the raiders that returned north. The leader that I saw had a deformed head and double rows of feet, and I think six fingers. If these are the ones at Fort Mountain then we would be best served to stay away from the summit."

"All I know is that if we do any trading for provisions it will be with those that live along the base of the mountain."

I expected there was more to the story. We continued toward the mountains and were happy not to encounter anything weird like strange lights and the hairy men. The foliage was different than the Enchanted Valley, and in some cases we had to hack our way into a tunnel so that we could walk through them. They were beautiful but annoying.

The first human that we encountered was a hunter following a deer. We didn't stop to talk, but he did point us in the direction of Fort Mountain. That night we camped on a ridge, and could faintly see the lights of fires from what we hoped would be some kind of village. We needed provisions for our push to Etowah and ultimately The Great Sea.

Chapter 4
Fort Mountain

It didn't take us long to reach the village that we had spotted last night. Some young boys spear fishing in a creek pointed us to the hut of one of the village elders. His home was easy to see as it sat on somewhat of an elevated mound. This would be a feature that would increase as we made our way south. We found two men talking out back and introduced ourselves.

"We are travelers Kolman and Ahki. Kolman has stopped here a few times on his way to his tribe the Duhare by the Great Sea."

Welcome travelers. My name is Eyota and let us sit in my lodge so that we may talk. I have food and drink if you are hungry and thirsty after your voyage."

The hut of Eyota was huge with a pointed roof. Like other huts of our people there was ample room in the roof for smoke to clear yet a structured space so that rain would stay out. This house was mostly made of mound grass. Eyota said they were making more wattle and daub house as the climate was getting colder because of the dragon from the sky. I also noticed a few stilt houses.

"You have come from the north. Is the weather getting colder there as well?"

"I'm afraid it is and is the main reason that I am heading to the land of the Duhare with Kolman."

"I must warn you that our neighbors on top of the mountain are becoming increasingly hostile. They seem to be running out of food and have taken up raids on our food stores at night. We have posted guards at our food bins at night to try and discourage any thievery. I'm sure you've heard of the Allegewi. Some call them the moon eyed people for their white eyes and the fact that they come out mostly at night. They live mostly in caves and have constructed a wall of stone higher than two men. The young warriors here have talked of storming the mountain and driving them out for good."

"Good luck Eyota. We have had some encounter with them in the north, so I know it won't be easy."

We thanked Eyota for his hospitality, and had probably the best sleep of our trip. Fort Mountain huts were bigger, but like ours they had cots built in all along the walls..The next few days were going to be some trading, and some final preparation to Etowah and then the Great Sea. We also had a chance to talk to some of the natives, and their stories about the Allegewi were all quite similar.

The day before we left was a worrisome time for me. I kept thinking about the Allegewi and Eyotas mention of a final assault on their stronghold on top of the mountain. Eyota asked us if we had enough provisions for our journey and I thanked him and said we were ready to go. For his hospitality I asked him if I could do him a favor. If they were to assault the top they would need current information. He said he would be grateful, but that I would be putting my life in danger. I told him it would be quick, and that he should tell Kolman that I would be back before the setting sun. If not he should expect the worse.

I decided to take a route that would put me to the side of their massive wall. If I was lucky I could tell Eyota about a route that they could use and not attack the wall directly in front. The movement up the mountain was slow, as I had decided to stay off any obvious paths. When I reached the summit what Eyota had described was in front of me. The wall was almost as high as three men, and only one small entrance that I could see. I had marked my path from the village and looked for natural markings to help guide Eyota near the entrance.

The daylight was fading fast, as it had taken me much longer to climb the mountain than I had expected. A trip down the mountain at night would be a dangerous trek so my plan was to take my blanket and find a warm spot for the night. The moon was full and the light was bright, yet I was unfamiliar with the terrain and I didn't wanted to risk being spotted by any scouts the moon-eyed people might send out.

Climbing up the mountain had tired me out, and it didn't take long for me to fall asleep. Some loud shouts brought to my senses and from my hiding spot I could make out a group that was leaving the wall. With the bright moon they had only one torch, and it was a sight I shall never forget. Some kind of

priest with antlers was leading a procession of people toward a clearing. He was carrying what I soon discovered was a severed head. No doubt a prisoner from the village that was captured after one of their raids. I began to understand why Eyota and his people wanted to drive these moon-eyed people from the area.

The shaman headed to a rock altar and proceeded to bash the severed head against the rock. A natural grove in the rock filtered the blood into a small stone cup. Blood and brains were mixed with sweat on the face of the priest. He brought out a large war club to finish the job. I had seen enough and didn't even stick around long enough to see what happened to the cup of blood.

Quietly I made my way back to my hiding spot. I had the choice of two moves, and I wasn't quite sure which one to take. The easiest way was to use the moonlight to work my way back down the mountain. My curiosity however got the best of me, and I took the foolhardy choice of entering the way where the shaman party had exited. I didn't see any guards and my plan was to get it and get out before the party returned. The chanting was still going on so I made my move.

There were small ledges on the inside of the wall, apparently where some kind of sentry was used during the day. This would be good information for Eyota if he decided to attack. I had heard that these people lived in caves so it wasn't surprising to find both manmade and natural caves. Some were small, and some had smoke coming out of them, so I naturally stayed away from the occupied ones. A larger one was just to my right, and even though I wasn't going to enter, something forced me to take a look inside.

What I saw haunts me to this day. My first glance caught some hunting tools. They were the black flint and obsidian knives used for butchering animals. Some still seemed to have blood glistening "on the blade. A small oil lamp gave limited sight, but it was just enough to send me scurrying back to the wall entrance. Just behind the knives were a pile of bones that gave me an idea of what they were butchering. They must be desperate for food as what I saw behind the bones were human skulls. They must be running out of food.

With this last bit of information I made my way back down the mountain. Eyota could use this information in his plan of attack. If they were weak they might be easier targets. I made my way to the spare hut that they made for us and waited for the rising sun. They had no rising sun ceremony so I hurried my way to Eyota's hut.

"Eyota, I'm sorry to bother you this morning, but I have some valuable information. I made a dangerous trip to the wall last night. After watching a human sacrifice I found a cave with human bones. I think they're running out of food."

"That seems to make sense Ahki. It seems they live by different rules. It also explains why people that disappear around here never return and their bodies are never found. We need to make sure that our people are made aware of this. It may scare them into staying closer to the village. We are in the process of building a stockade, and maybe this will encourage our people to finish it quicker."

"If they are running out of food then finishing the stockade will protect you if they decide to attack. I'm not a warfare expert, but I have seen my share of fights, and the weaker your opponent then the better your chances of survival. As long as these people remain on top of the mountain you will be in constant fear of them capturing and sacrificing your people. I would wait a few days and then organize an attack. I left markers on how to get up the mountain to the wall."

"Thank you Ahki. Kolman tells me that you are leaving today. I sorry that we don't have much in the way of provisions for your trip. It seems this colder weather has driven some of the game south. I don't know if you have plans to return to the Enchanted Valley, but if you do make sure you pay us a return visit."

After the usual farewells and thank you I returned to the hut to see if Kolman was ready for our voyage. He wasn't too concerned about our lack of food as he said the Etowah were the best fishermen that he had ever encountered. They had an elaborate system of dams and devices that funneled fish into their large supply of wicker baskets.

Chapter 5

Seamus

The next few weeks would be the toughest part of our journey to the sea. The hardest part was moving on foot to a place where we could obtain a boat. It of course did us no good now as we would need to pass Etowah before we could reach the river systems that led to the sea. The good news is that Kolman had a good relationship with the Etowah people and he was confident that we could obtain enough dry fish to continue our journey. We would be passing through some dangerous swampy area that contained some game, but also had poisonous snake like and gar like critters. I was familiar with the snakes that rattled, but some of the other creatures Kolman mentioned were strange to me.

The journey to Etowah was somewhat easy. Thank goodness it was a short journey, as we were unable to acquire much in the way of food from Fort Mountain. I nightly had dreams about the pale mountain people who were driven to the point of eating human flesh. My fear was that they were starting to enjoy the taste. Kolman and I on the other hand were living primarily off of roots and berries.

The Etowah village was one of the most beautiful villages that I had ever seen. It had no stockade or defensive walls so it was safe to say that these people lived in relative safety. There were however no mounds or any other kind of ceremonial areas. The main living areas were next to a small river. A river that they had turned into a place of continuous fish catching.

They had at least two rock dams that slowed the flow of the river, and in the places where the water came through they had platforms for the placement of wicker baskets. This river was so plentiful that it didn't take long for anyone to have a basket full of fish. The other impressive part of the village was their fish drying stations.

The fish drying racks consisted of large poles that were twice the length of a man. There were four poles on each side that acted as supports for three long fish holders. The total number of fish that they could dry at one time was over one hundred. The two most common catches were the whisker fish that I was familiar with, and a yellow colored fish that was the better tasting of the two.

Our stay at Etowah was short, and we were able to obtain through trade enough dried fish that should sustain us until we got to the river systems that would take us to the sea. We were soon to pass through some dangerous critter lands, and a full stomach would be necessary to pass through this region quickly.

Our first few days were calm with decent weather. It was when we entered the swampy land that our good luck began to change. We encountered on of the gar like creatures, and though he was slow he forced up into a run, and I unfortunately tripped and lost our fish supply in the murky water. From then on we divided our food supplies between the two of us just in case a similar incident would occur.

We tried and tried to locate the fish bag, but it seemed that the swamp had simply swallowed it up. Finally we came to the realization that it was lost, and that our next food source would need to be one that we caught ourselves. After just about a day of walking through the swamp, we finally came to a small island in the middle of all this muck. We completed a small lean to, and began to search for anything edible.

Our first few attempts were unsuccessful until Kolman almost stepped on our dinner. It was the snake that rattled. While Kolman stared it down I was able to grab and decapitate the snake with my obsidian knife. I had never eaten snake before, and Kolman constructed a slanting stick near our fire. The juices of the snake were popping and crackling and Kolman removed it from the fire. My ravenous hunger caused me to burn my mouth, and the speed at which I ate the snake made me throw up my first few bites. From then on I slowed down and enjoyed a highly satisfying meal.

The good news was that we were now entering the great river system that reached all the way to the sea. Kolman explained that his people lived north of this river system, and that we could reach their village by moving north along the Great Sea. Our plan now was to make contact with one of the boat builders that lived along the major river that Kolman called the Altamaha.

I was down to my last quartz crystal, and hopefully that would be enough for a small canoe for the both of us. Kolman had dealt with these people before. He called them the Maya, and he said that their leaders talked of their movement north from the mountains that belched fire. He said they were a race of people whose lands ranged far to the south to the land of turquoise blue water. Maybe my turquoise crystal would peek their interest.

Kolman said he knew these people had dugout canoes, since he was privileged to watch a large tree that was cut down and turned into what they called a dugout canoe. After spreading tobacco all around the tree as a sacrament, they proceeded to halve the tree, and to begin the process of hoeing out and burning out the log.

"If we're lucky Ahki, we will be able to obtain a smaller two man canoe. At the bottom of the tree they want the Maya place a girdle of mud and straw to about the height of a man's head. This protected the entire tree from burning down as they only wanted to burn the bottom part so the tree would fall down."

"Kolman I've seen a few huts here that use that mud and straw mixture for their walls."

"You shall see many more as we head south. To finish my story, once the fire was placed at the base of the tree, sticks with stone points were used to make the tree fall. The big trees fell easily as their weight did most of the work. They used the bark from these big trees to roof their huts."

"Was that the end of the process, the use of fire inside and out?"

"Almost. The last step which I think preserved it and kept it from cracking was the rubbing down of the canoe using bear grease."

Kolman told me more things about the dugout canoe process, and more about the somewhat secretive Maya. He said they had a larger village named Itsa-ya or Place of the Maya. They were most famous for their irrigation projects in the northern mountains near Fort Mountain which included ways to irrigate their crops in the valleys below.

We were successful in getting a dugout that would take us upon these vast river systems to the sea. These rivers were full of fish and we never went hungry. The types of water critters began to change and we were ever on the watch for the largest of the snakes in these rivers. On occasion we would see them swimming by our canoe and sometimes they seemed almost as long as our boat.

The only encounter happened when we were camped one night. We hand found the entrails of some animal that had died and decided to use the remains for bait. The fishing hole was a good place for the whisker fish and we proceeded to drop our lines in the hole and go looking for firewood. We had collected a bundle when we heard an awful commotion. A large snake had attached itself to a fish on ur line. We decided to go hungry for a while and quickly cut the line.

The rest of our trip was uneventful. The closer to the sea we got the more bizarre water creatures we would encounter. Some were familiar, others seemed to be variations of those I had encountered in the creeks to the north. One tasty treat was an animal that had claws like the crawfish in our creek. His body however was round, and Kolman made a nice stew of them in one of his pots.

Days passed and Kolman told me that we were getting close to his village. He said it was not directly on the great sea, but was by fresh water, and there was easy access by boat to the great water. We were unsuccessful fishing for the last few days, so the site of smoke hopefully meant a village and some good food.

Most of the smoke was coming from the largest structure in the village. I was surround by a small river of water. To access it we had to cross a small bridge that was just barely big enough for one person. Kolman said we would proceed to the large hut and meet the clan chief.

After we crossed the bridge we were greeted by clan members who knew Kolman. There was lots of communal hugging mixed into a language that I did not understand. Kolman could speak my language and his, and he explained to me that he would let me know what people were saying when we reached the hut of the clan leader. I was nervous about meeting the chieftain, and that feeling was

intensified by their war dogs. They were larger than any dog I had ever seen, and they had to be checked by their owners less we get attacked by these large animals.

The scene before me was a large village with plenty of children running from place to place. Most campfires seemed to be inside the huts. A large pen or stockade contained what looked like a herd of deer. Kolman had explained to me that these were not exactly deer, and were used primarily for their milk, and the food that they called cheese.

Men in the clan wore cloth that went all the way to their toes. They wore no shirts, but their upper bodies were covered in pictures and symbols. The men also had what Kolman called a hairy face called a beard. Taller than me, they were quite a sight with their long hair and pictured bodies.

We headed toward the largest of the huts that had a huge hole in the center of the roof that let smoke out. There were other openings around the structure that I'm sure served as ventilation in the warmest of days. Animal skins were also hung over many of these openings. They served as protection during some of the heavy rain that Kolman mentioned in his stories.

Entering the chief's lodge we were greated by the leader himself. Seamus was almost as tall as two men with the pictures that I had mentioned before. His beard and hair were bright red, and his hair seemed to flow to the floor. His wife and five children were eating around a firepit that contained large holders that looked like dogs.

Kolman explained to me that he was going to tell Seamus of our journey, and of my desire to stay here and experience The Great Sea. Seamus spoke for some time then Kolman explained to me what he had said.

"Seamus welcomed us and was curious to hear more about our story. He addressed your staying here with the idea that you could help out and be a productive member of the village. I explained to him your heroism and how you tried to save Kyana. He wanted you to tell some of your story. And why did you take on such a perilous journey?"

I tried to answer the best I could, but honestly I wondered myself why I would take such a journey. This was not like the journey from the White River back to the Enchanted Valley. This one would no doubt find me finishing my life story on the shores of The Great Sea.

Kolman said it was time to eat, and I immediately knew why this area was famous for its food. Scores of fish were brought out on wooden planks. Small pots of stew with sea animals were presented to us. Some of the critters reminded me of the pincher fish of the north. Many were shell creatures like fresh water clams but much larger.

We finished our meal with the milk of their deer. Again they were not like northern deer, and they used the milk primarily for the food they called cheese. After the meal Seamus stood up for some kind of prayer. Seamus was almost twice the size of our people with long red hair. His body was covered with strange pictures of different colors. I thanked him for the meal and Kolman then took me to his quarters. They were similar to northern huts, but were off the ground and had lots of holes for ventilation.

Chapter 6
Fishing Trip

I wasn't accustomed to sleeping in late, but these people had different customs, and they did not have the sun rising ceremony like we did. They also had funerary ceremonies that were different. No mounds were present in the area, and Kolman had told me that they buried bodies in the ground, but removed the head so that the spirit could escape. After a few days the head was reburied with the rest of the body. Strange.

Kolman was having what they called cheese for breakfast and I joined in.

"As you could tell from yesterday's meal we look to the sea for much of our food. Seamus wondered if you could join us on a trip tomorrow to the north as we are looking to fill our baskets withfish. Most of our people use nets and spears but Seamus was impressed with your bow and arrow andwas hoping that you would join us."

I agreed and spent the rest of the day working on my gear to get it ready for the fishing journey. The afternoon meal wasn't as lavish as the one where I met Seamus , but

I was quickly starting to like the many different varieties of sea creatures that provided them with food. In the afternoon Kolman took me on a stroll through the village where I met some of his people. They were a very colorful group what with their large hunting dogs and the number of people with red hair.

The children were very healthy and happy as were most of the villagers. One of the people he introduced me to caught my eye from the beginning. Her name was Shona and she was grieving over the loss of her mate. He was killed in a fishing trip in just about the same location as where we are going to tomorrow. I knew there would be more than the usual danger on this trip.

Most of the danger would be with wild animals. Big cats and bears and serpent type animals were of course where most of the danger would lie, but Mother Nature had plenty of surprises herself with most of them being different from those of the Enchanted Valley. One story that was particularly chilling was the one about the fisherman swallowed up by the earth. It was somewhat similar to the time I was caught in the mud at Pottery Point. The only difference was that this phenomena was a deep hole that swallowed up things and people.

The next morning we packed up enough things for a few days trip. I had my bow with rope tied to the arrows so that I could retrieve any fish that I might shoot. Wicker baskets on a sled were pulled by some camp dogs. We didn't take a lot of food since we were hoping to survive on shellfish and anything else that we could catch. Jugs of fresh water were also important as the water of The Great Sea was salty and undrinkable.

I was excited more about seeing The Great Sea for the first time than the actual hunt. Kolman said that we would hunt the small rivers and estuaries before we reached The Great Sea. He also said that his people had hid a few boats with what he had called sails at a spot that was safe from small storms. Nothing he said was safe anywhere during what he called the death storms.

I'm not sure if it was the smell or the sound that I experienced first. We had traversed so many shallow areas that had been marked by Kolman's people, that the sound and the smell of the great sea took me by surprise. But there it was, the blue water was everywhere. I was standing on a sandy bank with large sea grass waving all around me. I fell on my bottom and was in awe of the spectacle before me. Birds with large beaks were flying in formation. Occasionally one would peel off and dive down to catch a fish.

The group was heading to an area where they had hid a larger boat, one that had what they called a sail. The plan was for a few to do the fishing, and the rest of us would be ready to clean the catch once they returned to shore. They had hid the boat in an area close to a small river that entered the sea. Entering the sea by the way of the river would protect them from some of the waves that battered the shore. Kolman said the waves today were below average, so the boatman should have an easy entrance and planned to stay only a short time. We would clean the fish and collect the shellfish we had gathered and head home. We would probably stay all night in a dry area and head home the next day.

Those that remained on the beach positioned themselves on a large pile of sand to watch the spectacle of the boat leaving the river and heading into the open sea. On their sail they had painted a large cross with a circle at the top. Kolman stayed with me and told me that the sea was unusually calm, and that sometimes they didn't go out because of the high waves.

Kolman said that they were fishing for some of the bigger fish, but would stay away from the monster fish, some whose teeth we had found earlier in the day buried in the sand. He said they had never seen a fish that big, but were always wary and never left the sight of the shore. Some of us were tired and dozed off while the fishermen continued their quest. We had watched them haul aboard one or two larger big mouthed fish and were confident we would soon be making our way back home.

We were all startled by a blood curdling scream and instinctively looked to the boat to see what was wrong. The fishermen were fine so we checked the beach only to find someone running and screaming. He fell and the screaming stopped. Some of us went to his aid to find out what was going on. One of the large hard shell creatures with claws had attached himself to the man's private areas. He was moaning and most of us were laughing.

The day continued without incident and we were glad that the only injury so far was a man with pinched testicles. Just before the boat was coming ashore, another strange incident happened that luckily involved no injuries. I'm not sure if this creature was attracted by the fish already caught, but all of us were shocked by a large fish that jumped into the boat. It looked like it had a small log in front of its face, and the fishermen were lucky to get the creature back into the water with no one hurt.

We counted our blessings, and proceeded to prepare the catch for the journey home. Each fish was cleaned and some of the innards like the liver were kept for bait. The eatable parts were covered with salt that we had brought in our small sled. The fish were then covered in layers of cloth and put in a shady spot on the sled. Our goal was to make it inland far enough to find a dry and safe place to spend the night.

I've been more than lucky, and on this night my luck saved me from the fate of one of the

fishermen on the trip. That night we enjoyed a super fish meal around the fire, and retold the stories of the creature that jumped in the boat and the man who was attacked by the claw creature. Both were accompanied by lots of laughter thanks to the drinking of something they called honey wine, a drink made from the food of the stinging bees. It was of course sweet and so far it is my favorite drink.

Most of us retired early and were in a deep sleep when it happened. Cries of help and a large crashing noise took all of us out of a deep sleep. Small groups of us were sleeping underneath a few trees when the disaster occurred. The fire was still going so we lit torches to find out what was going on. The noise and the cries for help led me to a sight I'll never forget. The ground had collapsed and men were being sucked down into the hole. We were scared, but it seemed that we had pulled everyone out of the hole.

After everyone had calmed down we realized what had happened. The ground had collapsed into a large hole that had swallowed up everything, including the men who were sleeping on top of it. No one seemed to be injured until we took a count of who was here. One man was missing. We went back to the hole and even dropped torches into the hole. The flames went out of sight. His body was never found.

After an exhausting search we realized our efforts were futile. The elders in the group made sure everyone was present and they commenced to say a prayer of their tribe:

May there be a beautiful welcome for you in the home that you are going to.

You are not going somewhere strange.

You are going back to the home you never left.

May your going be sheltered and your welcome assured.

May your soul smile in the presence of your soul friends.

The trip back to the village was somber indeed. Many in the group talked about the wake that they would hold for the deceased. He was a younger clan member with no wife and whose parents had been gone for many years. They still knew that cousins and friends would want to stay up days drinking the honey drink and celebrating his life.

As we entered the village we were surprised by a funeral celebration. It was of course not our departed friend's as they knew nothing of this tragedy. It was a funeral for an older member of the clan. She was famous for her basket making and knowledge of plants that could be used for healing.

The clan were making their way to a funerary house..The body was covered in white fabric with darker pieces of cloth. Lighted oil lamps were placed around the body. Clay pipes filled with tobacco were placed around the room. Every male caller was expected to take at least one puff. The smoke kept evil spirits from finding the deceased.

Kolman explained to me what would happen in the next two or three days. We would be celebrating the passing of two clan members. Some of our people up north were buried in the ground, but down here digging two deep in the earth caused the water to fill the hole. These people here would place the body on a platform and send the body in smoke form to the otherworld.

I forget most of the revelry the next few days. The honey wine flowed like water and I made quick friends by bringing out the spiked leaf plant. Some of the clan members had flutes and drums and the wake was highlighted by these frenzied dances of love for the deceased. I slept it off in Kolman;s hut and when I woke up which seemed to be days later he told me the funeral celebration was over.

Chapter 7
Death Storm

The next few months went quickly, and Kolman began talking about deadly storms that came from the sea. He said that the last few years had been calm, and he blamed this on the cooler weather. It seemed the world had cooled since the "fiery dragon" had appeared in the northern skies. One evening around the campfire he told stories of their strength and their danger.

"This land of ours offers our people the fruits of the sea. But as we found out on our last fishing trip, it also show us how dangerous Mother Nature can be. The sea creatures that eat men inhabit the sea, and serpents live in our rivers. But the most fearsome arm of nature is the death storm. Not the rains or thunder, but the rising of the water and their deadly winds. In the last storm we were able to survive, but I fear larger storms are out there, and our elders have talked about death storms that can destroy man and beast. We must forever be vigilant and be prepared to head inland to get away from the rising of the sea."

Now I realized why the homes were built on poles. If the sea did rise as high as Kolman predicted, then being above the waters would be the only way to survive. The walls of the huts were heavy with dried mud, but the roofs were fragile and needed to be reinforced. Workers spent days placing heavy ropes over them. These ropes would hopefully keep some of the roof intact in case of heavy winds.

I helped in any way I could, and sometimes it just involved taking water to the workers. Shona was also helping carry water, and I enjoyed her many stories of her life with the Duhare. She didn't remember much about her trip across the sea, but she did have lots of stories about how they made friends with people who were already here. Their arrival was not always easy, as some of the locals thought they were demons, what with their size and red hair and painted bodies.

We had finished carrying water to the workers when a scout from a friendly clan nearby asked permission to speak with Seamus. From what we found out later he and his friends were fishing in the Great Sea when they noticed an oncoming storm. From the darkness and the raising and lowering of the water he feared it was a death storm. We had finished with the homes anyway, so our next job was to prepare for a trip inland. We each prepared enough food and water to last us for a day or two. These storms could last a longtime, depending on their size as some were bigger and some smaller.

The news from the scout wasn't the only warning that we had. The obvious warning from Mother Nature was the darkening of the skies and the picking up of the wind.

These two events were enhanced by the actions of the animals. The domestic deer ran around their pens and tried to escape. The camp dogs also began a series of howling that would have woken up the dead. We had planned to take some of the animals with us, males and females. The most alarming warning seemed to come from the heavens. A round white light appeared off the coast and stayed there for some time. It blinked a few times then was gone.

The wind began to pick up, and water from our river began entering the village. The camp dogs were hooked to sleds that would carry provisions for the few days that we would need in the interior. Kolman and I stayed close together, and some of the parents tied themselves to their children with rope. The last groups of scouts were carrying torches through the darkness and screaming cries of warning to everyone that we were leaving.

As we made our way inward we made sure that we kept our distance from the river. The sea water was now backing up and it was no place to be near. Objects were whirling by as we made our way north. A whirlwind made its way up the river, and it reminded me of the twister storms of my homeland. The objects were flying furiously now. A man behind us let out a blood curdling scream and fell to the ground. Next to him was a large clam shell that had struck him in the head. We wiped off the blood and helped him to his feet.

The forest was getting thicker, and many sought shelter under the larger trees. This proved to be a bad idea as many of the trees were old, and their dead limbs were being tossed to the ground by the wind. A huge branch narrowly missed us but one of the camp dogs was not so fortunate. A large limb stuck him in the head and he died instantly. Normally these people would bury their dogs, butthere was no time for any burials. We had to make the prepared shelters before dark. Those who hadbeen in such storms said that after the worse winds a lull would occur then a second round of winds would happen.

The rains were now coming sideways, and we made sure that we stayed away from dry creek beds that at any time could turn into a raging flash flood. Kolman had been to the site before, and he knew from the terrain that we were getting closer. The land was getting somewhat hilly, and I assumed that the storm shelters were on higher ground away from any flood waters.

Shelter number one loomed ahead of us, and it was formidable as not only a storm shelter, but could be used as a defense position in case of any raider type attacks. At the present time the Duhare were on friendly terms with their neighbors, but that situation could change due to hunting ground squabbles and the like. But if we needed to use it for that purpose, this place would be ideal.

These shelters were adequate, and were already stocked with what we would need for a few days stay. Runners would occasionally check the shelters to make sure that there was fresh food and water. The storms only occurred during a certain part of the year, so the Duhare made sure these shelters were ready before the devil storms occurred.

The rain had started to subside, and the elders said these storms sometimes contained a lull, but would start back up with the same amount of force. During this time

Seamus had sent two young runners to check on the village. He sent them on a path that would take them away from the river, and away from the flooding. They left in the morning and had not returned that evening. This was disturbing to Seamus as the wind and rain had picked up again. When only one returned his fears were confirmed. While checking the huts, the sea had risen sharply to where it was entering the huts. One of the runners was caught in a rogue wave and swept out to sea. His body was never found. Seamus said a funeral would be held later.

We stayed there for a couple of days until the driving rain stopped. Our route back took us far away from the rivers as they were flooding at an alarming rate. The carnage of the village was something we will never forget. Those in charge of the domestic deer had let them go to fend for themselves during the storm. They had now returned and the herders set about repairing their pens. Some of the grain storage bins had been destroyed and we were all hoping that we had enough to take us through the colder months. The growing season was longer down here so chances were that we would make it.

The most striking thing was the debris. Huts that were not well put together were smashed against the trees that survived. One of the camp dogs had been killed by one of these fallen trees. The Duhare had an area where some of their ancestor's ashes were placed with crosses and a circle running through the top. Some of these had been destroyed and it would take months to repair what they called their cematery. In fact the whole village would take months to repair, but the most important thing was the small amount of loss of life.

CHAPTER 8

SHONA AND THE SMELLY MONSTER

The next few months were extremely tiresome for all of us. The repairs to the physical structures would be the easiest to repair. The mental anguish caused by stress and the loss of personal things would leave a lasting scar. Some of the youngest ones would begin to cry during a strong wind or heavy rain. The older ones began talking about moving further inland. The rest of us continued to repair physical structures and assure others that we have survived these storms in the past and will continue to do so.

During this time I began a relationship with a woman that I hope will continue for the rest of this level of existence. Shona and I were about the same age and worked together on consoling those older than us, and trying to convince the younger ones to stay here and tough it out. It was during this time that we began helping each other. For me it was Shona trying to convince me that if my wife wanted to be with me she would have stayed in The Enchanted Valley. For Shona it was me trying to convince her that she could not have changed the events that led to her husband's death, whether it would have been convincing him to stay or going on the fishing trip herself.

At first it was simple idle conversation, but it first developed into an understanding of things about this earth that we both enjoyed. She enjoyed fishing as much as I did, and we both enjoyed searching the swampy areas for medicinal plants. The storm had destroyed the hut that contained most of these stores, so Shona and I volunteered to replenish the stores. We also discovered that we both had a sense of humor and enjoyed story telling. On one beautiful night with only the light from oil lamps illuminated the room. We were both startled by the lamps increasing their light only to discover that it was the rising of the sun. We had talked all night.

We began making trips to the swampy areas to collect herbs for our new medicine hut. The first we picked was one of the more common ones. I called it sharp I grass for its sharp spiky leaves.

It not only was edible, but seemed to cure stomach problems. Lizard's Tail was another common plant near our camp. It was great for insect bites and to reduce fever. The Rattlesnake Plant was a favorite of us older clan members. When taken as a powder it seemed to help with the aches and pains of old age. As far as pain was concerned the best were the plants grown from my seeds that I brought with me. They were the spiky leave plants that sometimes grew as tall as a man. The Sun Plant is another one that we collected and its yellow flower opens up at midday. The root of this plant contained a powerful pain killer.

Two of the plants that the Duhare used also grew up North. I was familiar with ginseng and sassafras. They used ginseng and sassafras in a tea. Ginseng is especially good for certain types of sprains and leg injuries. Sassafras is good for sneezing illnesses and headaches. We collected our last batch of these herbs and were getting ready to head back to the village.

This particular day was warmer than most. Since the fiery dragon the climate of the earth has seemed to cool. We were walking near some swampy roots when in a darker part of the swamp something seemed to move. It was crouched down and seemed to be eating some kind of melon. At first we couldn't tell the size but we could certainly smell the critter. The smell was that of a dirty dog that suddenly got caught in a rainstorm.

When it stood up it reminded me of one of the hairy men. I had never seen one in broad daylight and this one was impressive. The height and weight of this creature was that of two men. It was covered in thick fur and again smelled like a dirty wet dog. When it spotted us it let out a wail and dissappeared deeper into the swamp.

We thought we had seen the last of the creature, but just in case he was still around we decided to head back to the safety of the camp. None of these creatures had ever been sighted close to camp. In fact the only dangerous critters close to camp were the larger snakes and what the Duhare called alligators. The most dangerous creature in these parts was a cousin of the big cat that we had killed on our winter hunt up north.

I'm not sure if the hot weather enhanced our scent or this was just an unlucky day for us, but the stinky monster wasn't the last critter that we encountered that day. We were in an area of taller grass and to our left we noticed a small key deer popping up through the tall grass as it made its way in a panic mode toward a grove of trees. It didn't take long for us to see why the deer wanted to hide among the trees. The big cat had tired the deer out and was steadily gaining ground on the poor creature. Right before the deer entered the grove the cat suddenly stopped. He had given up chasing the deer and was now moving in a different direction. The direction was toward us.

Shona wanted to run, but I told her that was the worst thing that we could do. We let the cat do her slow cat like approach while we tried to figure out our next move. Shona wanted to hide in the grass, but I decided on a move that had worked on bears. Shona crawled onto my shoulder and we tried to make ourselves bigger than we actually were.

With Shona on my shoulder, the cat stopped in his tracks. This shocked both of us, and what happened next shook us to the core. Out of the grove of trees sprang the stinky hairy man. I was amazed how fast a creature of that size could move. With one giant leap he was on the back of the big cat and they tumbled together through the swampy grass. The cries of the cat and the screams of the hairy man echoed through the swamp. The cat was trying to get to the back of the stinky man, and the stinky man was looking like he was trying to strangle the cat. He finally grabbed the cat's head, and what happened next was especially gruesome. By pulling the cat's upper jaw and lower jaw of the cat at the same time with a powerful thrust the cat's head almost left his body. The screaming stopped and as quickly as he came the hairy man ran back to the grove of trees. He made one last scream and then disappeared. Shona and just stared at each other and couldn't believe what we had just witnessed.

After a night of telling this tale, Shona and I settled in with the routine of what seemed to be the life of a married couple. We didn't marry, but the two of us seemed destined to be with each other. Both of us had knowledge of the medicinal plants, and began making an extra hut where we could dry and cure plants for healing, and sometimes for food.

The shed was smaller than the normal hut that we used for sleeping. Like the living quarters it was on stilts to protect us from rain and snakes and the like. There were lots of creepy crawlies in this area so close to the sea. After the shed was completed Shona and I began to talk about what plants we would need for the hut. Again most were medicinal but some were edibles and ceremonial plants that were mostly smoked. These people didn't smoke as much as my people to the north, but I introduced them to what my people called kinnikinnick, a mixture of herbs and leaves and bark.

Some of the younger men and women were the farmers and they harvested anything from squash to wild rice. I gave them some of my sunflower seeds, and they were happy to add those to their wild garden. We had used mushrooms for ceremonies, but these people collected them as a food source. I was not familiar with wild rice and Shona took me on a trip to collect some of this tasty grain.

"We will need a small boat and we need to make sure that the boat owners will receive their fair share."

"Explain to me Shona what we will need and how we go about collecting the grain."

"Well we first need to find a stand of the grain. I'll let you paddle and I will use these wooden sticks to knock the grain into our baskets. You can use a push pole as we glide through the stand of plants. I will use the sticks to gently dislodge the grain. Some of the grain will fall back into the swamp and will help grow a new stand next year."

We spent the next few moons traveling to the swamp to retrieve plants, and to gather some of the foods like swamp rice. Our shed was getting fool of medicinal plants and a few foodstuffs. I had built rafters for many of the medicinal plants. In these rafters I hung many of the plants to dry, especially a few plants that were smoked. The Duhare were not smokers, but they became accustomed to my spiky leaf plant, both as a medicine and as ceremonial plant at their feasts. Shona and I never encountered a big cat or stinky swamp man again. We did have one other experience together that was stranger and one that could have been much more dangerous.

Chapter 9
The Others

Both of our cultures had in their stories and legends, the presence of supernatural entities that crossed our paths on occasion . on one evening around the fire I had retold the story of my forest experience with enchanted beings. They had seemed to be able to stop time and like my friends to the north most of the Duhare blamed my experience on ceremonial mushrooms. The Duhare had stories that seemed to me as crazy as my forest story.

The next morning after the story telling, Shona told me that she had experiences and probably would continue to encounter not forest people but sky people. She even took me to a spot in a clearing that was some distance from the village and was a secret spot that she had not told anyone about. She was afraid that if she told anyone that they would think that she was crazy.

"It's just up ahead Ahki. Look at this grassless circle. It will take us around 200 steps to Complete the circle. Do you feel any different after this walk."

"I feel dizzy and somewhat energized."

"I've been to this place a few times when I was sick and felt recovered after this kind of walk.

Shona explained to me that in a dream she was told that this circle was from the sky people. Those ancestors that brought us to this world and who still stop in to check on us and the planet. I didn't think much of this until many moons later when we both had an experience together.

Just at the edge of the swamp, where there was little or no water, was a small clearing that was used as a grazing area for some of the wild deer. We normally stayed away from it as it was also frequented by some of the predators like bears and big cats. On this day the suns brightness glowed from an object that was pretty much dead center in the middle of the clearing. It looked like a boat with a closed top. Shona said it reminded her of something called a chariot that the old people talked about as a legendary war machine. It was as long as the length of three men and was as tall as two men.

We were frightened by its strangeness and were ready to backtrack our steps when the creature appeared. It was much smaller than us and did seem to have much of a mouth. With big eyes and a big head it reminded us both of a demon and we began to run. It spoke to us to try and reassure us that we need not be frightened. The weird thing was that we both heard the same thoughts in our mind and not aloud.

The creature assured us that they were repairing their boat and would soon be leaving. This was a sky boat and they were sky people. Their mission was to be stewards and watchers of the planet. They had brought hairy men from their place and were checking on them. They also said they were checking on other species to make sure that there was a balance of nature. They seemed to imply that we were safe from most of the creatures except a sea serpent that until now we thought was just a legend.

We remembered this after we woke up from being unconscious. We were in knee deep grass and immediately began worrying about predators. After we got to our feet we scurried back to the village and told no one about our encounter. This was not the only encounter that we would have with sky people and this one would turn out to be a little scarier.

Shona and I were getting a good reputation as healers, and on this day we were looking for ingredients that were part of a concoction that was more of a preventive medicine for the aches and pains of old age. Most of this drink consisted of seashell powder, seaweed, and blueberries. Not the tastiest of drink, but many swore about its healing properties.

We had also experimented with a variety of plants, and on this day we were collecting three different plants that we used for different reasons. One was forsythia. We used it as a fever reducer. Honeysuckle was one of our favorites and we used it as a pain reliever. Mint leaf not only made a tasty tea but was also used for chills and the like. Our final item on our list was the inside of the reed plant. It was probably our most effective pain reliever and fever reducer. But on this day we were so shaken by events that we only brought ourselves back to the village.

It was getting late and we had yet to complete our list, so we headed to an area of higher ground where we were hoping to find honeysuckle. The sky was getting dark and we thought we heard a slight humming noise. Over my shoulder a shadow appeared and at first I panicked and thought it was a return of a Thunderbird creature like the one we encountered in The Zone of Extraordinary Travel. But as the shadow grew larger I realized the object had no wings and was making just a slight humming noise. It was floating directly over our heads and began to descend just beyond some tall grass. Before it landed we could see that it was shaped like a spear or long canoe, and lights on the side looked like they contained the silhouettes of people.

We were speechless and frozen in our tracks. A door on the side opened and a ramp came silently out of the side of the object. A human like creature carrying a spear emerged from the craft. He was about the same size as Shona's people, but with none of the pictures on his body. He carried a spear that had a light on the end. Like the other creature, this one seemed to talk without moving his mouth. He said his name was Lu, and that they needed to repair their ship. On board the craft we could hear what seemed to be laughing and singing. He said he was from Hy Brasil, which made Shona gasp, and he quickly returned to his ship. It must not have taken long for his repairs, since the craft vanished at incredible speed

Shona and I returned to the medicine hut where she told me stories about Hy Brasil. She always thought that this island near her home was the place where gods lived. Lu didn't seem like a god, yet Shona said he was their people's god of war. What was strange she said that the god Lu also carried a spear, one that emitted lightening and fire and burning light.

She told me what she knew of this mysterious island. It was somewhere in the Great Sea between her homeland and the place that we now call home. Explorers told stories of inhabitants who looked like the men from the north. They were about the same size as the Duhare, but some were larger and their skins were pale and void of pictures. Legend has it that these creatures spoke of the land to the west which was more proof that the land we lived in existed.

Her father told her that these were star people. The island wasn't really as much an island as it was a base where they could live and study the people of this planet. Their mission was to protect the planet and all life including us. This explained many unusual things that I had seen or heard of. Even during the great storm that almost destroyed our village we had witnessed strange lights in the sky.

They spoke of an area near here called The Zone. It was different in that there were mountains and it was almost entirely void of water. This area was primarily used by them as a base. They also dropped off a few different plants and animals in the area. When asked about visiting the area they simply said that it was not safe. Some of the animals that they talked about were giant turtles and white snakes with red eyes.

Stories of flying objects also came from my homelands in the north. Objects that had three sides and lots of lights on the inside were reported by people that lived near Mound City. Some traders who frequented the area where the Deer River met the Great River spoke of an object that resembled what Shona and I saw. Twice they saw it move up the Deer River just above the tree line. It moved slowly and made little or no sound. The observers followed it from ridge line to ridge line until it disappeared just above the hills near Mound City.

My father had told me a story when I was a child. For most of my years I had believed it to be a story that parents told to their children to keep them in line. Behave or the star people will snatch you and take you away. He said it happened one day when he was hunting along the ridges near Far Point. He described them differently from the Hy Brasil creatures. One approached him and acted like he was lost. He had dark skin and dark eyes and strange shoes. He had coverings over his head and hands.

The creature told my father that he was part of an exploring party and that he got lost. He said he had lost an object that would take him back to his people. After he described the area where his friends were my father was able to take him back to his craft. The other creatures bowed and thanked him for bringing the other one back to the silver canoe. He also said that they would take children who misbehaved away from their parents. I now think this was one part of the story that was untrue.

CHAPTER 10
ALTAMAHA

Shona and I recovered from the star people stories only to be confronted by an even stranger story and one that possibly posed an even stronger threat. Most of the fishing trips had been to the north and although dangerous they did seem to be anything close to the danger we were going to face heading south. I knew from stories that this area was a natural man trap of deep water and mud. Boats were also in dangerous territory as whirlpool and eddies would sometimes form that could devour a small boat.

These natural earth features were nothing compared to the story of the creature. He was said to live in parts south and he was nothing like the largest critters we had encountered up north. The description of the creature was enough to scare anyone away from the trip south. It was described to be as long as four men with a long neck and a mouth full of sharp teeth. Reports also had it possessing a snakelike spiny tail. Some even said that it was green with glowing eyes. I had never even dreamed of such a creature.

I was invited on this particular trip but after these stories I was hesitant to say yes. Shona had heard all the stories and said she had no desire to go. She believed that actually every fishing trip south in the last few years was to capture or kill the creature. The creature she said would never be found. It was an expert at blending in with the surroundings and it had plenty of hiding spots. The only way that she thought that anyone could catch it was to catch it sunning itself on the banks of one of the local rivers.

Before I said yes or no I wanted to speak to an elder who had supposedly seen the creature. Shona directed me to the hut of an elder who said he would speak to me. A few had been shaken so much by the encounter that they refused to speak of the creature. .After a few greeting formalities the elder described his encounter.

"I was away from the rest of the group and was paddling close to the edge of the river. I had a net that would catch some of the smaller fish to use for bait. As a came around a bend in the river I saw the creature sunning itself on the bank. When it spotted me it rolled itself into the water. As it rolled I saw a whitish-yellow underbelly. When it swam away I could see a bony ridge on the top of its body. When it swam away I noticed it was using only front flippers. My hopes that it was gone were dashed when I saw it swimming toward me. It had a nose like the creature we call an alligator. Its scariest features were its large protruding eyes and a mouth full of sharp teeth. Fortunately for me that it swam under and capsized my boat close to the bank. I ran from the bank as fast as I could. I only lost my boat that day and not my life. The last think I remember was the sound of it hissing and bellowing."

I thanked the elder for his story and retold it to Shona. The hissing and bellowing part were not encouraging. The party were not leaving for a few days so I had plenty of time to give them an answer of whether or not I was going. In my final decision it was whether or not I wanted to risk my life one more time. But then again this body only had a few more trips left in it and this could be the trip of my lifetime.

Shona tried to convince me not to go. She said a man of my age should not be going on such a strenuous journey. My explanation to her was that very reason. My age dictated that this could be my last journey. There was something about the description of the creature that drove me on. It was one of a kind. It was ancient. Like me.

Preparation for the trip took almost a day. The usual fishing trip essentials like hooks and nets and baskets were present but the nets were different. We had our usual bait nets, but also a couple of nets big enough to catch a large sea creature. These must have been made especially for the monster. If the creature was truly that big I'm not sure I wanted anything to do with it.

Other essentials included food for the trip and medical supplies. Poultices and fish sinew were in my bag to cover and repair small cuts and injuries. Larger rope to be used to prevent someone from bleeding out were also in my bag. It seems that I was identified by some in the clan as the official healer.

On this trip I'm not sure that I wanted to be burdened with such a responsibility.

The poultice that I used were different from anything the Duhare had ever used. The one that I used was from a shaman up north. It was made primarily from the bark of the elder tree. Shona had made one for me from a plant that she called plantain. It was a plant that the Duhare also used for food, so I had to guard it to make sure a hungry member of our group didn't eat it before we had a chance to use it. It reminded me of a plant up north that we called paw paw. They were good to eat but I had never thought of using it as a poultice.

Other facets of the trip were somewhat interesting. Usually on a fishing trip the weapons were few and far between. Spears of course and just recently with my arrival a crude form of the bow and arrow were used. Like my fishing arrows they were attached to rope so that the smaller fish could be pulled in. With this trip I noticed some larger weapons which I assumed were for a creature that was as long as four men. These were of the strange hare material that was stronger than rock and could be attached to wooden poles. They were two hands big and consisted of a sharp point and an axe looking side. They were very effective in stabbing and slashing.

Another interesting part of the trip was the makeup of those who had volunteered. Most were male and most were young. There were a couple that stood out from the rest. One was the largest and oldest of all the males. He had long red hair and was covered with the picture like drawings that were common to the Duhare. They weren't really pictures as much as they were symbols. The most common one was circles within circles. They also had symbols of three lines that intertwined within each other.

I of course took my bow, and my prime weapon of choice. It was a knife that I had fashioned from the crystal cave of The Zone of Extraordinary travel. In the middle of its steam and hot water ponds was a cave full of gemstones. I fashioned the bluestone knife and used a deer antler for a handle. I also secured the sheath and knife to my body considering where we were going. The Altamaha region of swamps and small rivers would never give it up if dropped into its mud. This knife would come to save my life.

The only female of the group instantly reminded me of Kyana. She not only looked like Kyana, but she seemed to have similar interests. My bow seemed to intrigue her and after a few lessons I decided to let her use it on this trip. I still was haunted by the vision of Kyana slipping beneath the waves of the Great River and I was determined to stop this from happening to the girl I called the Brown One as her skin was much darker than hardly anyone in the clan.

The day we left we assembled near the great hall and received a prayer from Seamus. This would be our longest and most treacherous journey so we needed all the help we could get. The youngest of the group were hugging their wives and boasting of the predicting success for the journey. They promised to bring back great quantities of edible sea creatures. For this journey theye were also taking a few camp dogs that were not only huge but expert swimmers as well.

I gave Shona a hug and I thought I detected a tear in the corner of her eye. She begged me one more time not to go as she knew the danger of this journey. I waved goodbye as we headed over some sand dunes and marched toward the sea. It was a beautiful but windy day and we wore masks to protect us from the blowing sand. The dogs scouted ahead with their handlers. It was wasn't long before one came running back howling without his handler. It had a hard shelled sea critter with pincers attached to his nose. We all laughed and then helped him removed the creature. These creatures had succulent meat inside their shell but this one was too small to keep.

The first day was uneventful as we made our way along the coast. We stopped for the night as we were approaching a large bay and it would be too dangerous to attend a crossing by night. Our plan was to look for the shortest area to cross and then mark it for the return trip. We normally would ask help from the locals, but none were around for this trip. The area was a little too dangerous for permanent villages, but we did have a few who had made the trip before and they had a general idea of where the shortest point to cross was. As we bedded down for the night I was again amazed by the night sky and The Pathway of Departed souls. Would I be walking that path soon? I dosed off thinking that I had seen a light on the sea. Star people? I disappeared and I closed my eyes.

Scouts and the dogs left early the next day to look for the shortest spot to cross the bay to the other side. Those in camp had some dried fish and what the Duhare had called cheese. It was made from the deer of their camp animals that they called deer, but they weren't like normal deer. You couldn't keep normal deer in camp. The plan was to begin the crossing once the scouts had found and marked the spot. The boats that we had on sleds were few and couldI only hold two people. We would have to ferry people over one at a time.

I thought that this would take longer, but some of the young warriors crossed by means I had never even guessed at. The Duhare had special shields that were made of a normal than lighter wood. The shields was bowed in a way that the young men crawled on top of something that reminded me of a turtle shell. They started upstream and were able to paddle to the opposite shore.

This ended up taking most of the day, and once we were safely across we finished the day having a large fish feast and celebrating the fact that the crossing was a safe one. I'm not sure what caused the magical dream that not. It was probably the gluttony of the feast or the excess of the fermented drink of theirs. Most dreams are ones that I forget. The dreams that I do remember always have dead people in them. Are they coming back to visit me in my dreams? This one was graphic by the things that seemed to be scary moments in my life. There weren't many raiders, but the hairy man was obvious. The raiders were present as they killed two of the most important people in my life, my brother Neegosis and Kyana.

The next morning began with a light rain and we found what trees we could to fashion some kind of shelter using the boats. After the rain we began our journey south. Today we would spend the day doing what I called island jumping. The islands that hugged the coast were a better way of traveling for a variety of reasons. For one we didn't need to cross large bodies of water. We were heading to fishing grounds that had the reputation of being the richest on the coast. Our problem would be having enough men to bring the dried fish or shellfish home. The other advantage was a constant light wind that kept the biting bugs off. These were the same kind of bugs that had caused me to cover myself up north with mud and charcoal. These bugs were different in that they sometimes carried a deadly fever. The Duhare had lost a few people from this disease.

We decided that we had come as far as we liked and decided to make a semi-permanent camp. This camp would serve as our base of operation as well as a place to dry and get ready our catch for the trip back home. There were patches of driftwood that made excellent lean twos when covered with tall swamp grass. It also kept us out of the sun. Although temperatures had cooled in this reason because of the dragon in the sky, it still would make us red since I was used to it and the Duhare were fair skinned.

The first day at camp consisted of us doing some finishing touches and relaxing from the long coastal voyage. No major injuries and everyone was in good health. A plan was discussed that any sickness or injury would result in a trip home. The Duhare had a grape liquid that they had acquired on their trading missions to the north. I didn't bring any of the spiked leaf in smoking form because of a worry about us not being level headed. I did have a paste that I made that was a good pain reliever for injuries.

The grape drink proved to be worse than the spiked leaf. Normally the Duhare had sentries to watch for any camp intruders. Our only sentries were the few camp dogs that we brought along and the fact that they were such good watch dogs may have been another reason that our sentries went to sleep. They did their job but not before we were awakened by their howls and a crash and some screams. The crash was a lean two falling over and the screams were the men whom were unfortunately inside and trying to sleep.

After the initial surprise the camp came to life to see if anyone was hurt. Thank goodness the men were alive, but one of the camp dogs was missing. With our torches we noticed some strange tracks that looked like something had slithered up and then vanished in one of the tributaries. It was too dark to follow but we decided to wait until morning to follow the tracks.

We lost the trail after a while due to the terrain and the fear of running into a nest of the more dangerous critters in the area. Most were snakes, but some were the larger blunt nose reptiles that reminded me of the monster that my brother and I ran into on the Deer River. The group decided to return to base camp and to gather up and smoke enough sea creatures for the trip home. We had plenty of shellfish and redfish to harvest, and our stay here could be limited to a few moons.

The process of smoking and preparing the catch for transport was somewhat boring. It involves salting and drying and smoking. The fish were placed on racks and some of the shellfish were in wicker baskets. The Duhare had learned this method from some of the local tribes who had been doing this long before the Duhare arrived. Some of the younger men were assigned to keep the fire going. Young men are especially prone to boredom and this is what happened to one of the smokers. His friend had spent part of the day complaining and then around midday had wandered off. We had spent many an hour warning the young ones not to wander off by themselves.

With the treacherous terrain, and the fact that many were unfamiliar with the terrain, we decided to arrange our search parties in groups of three. My group decided to head toward one of the larger bodies of water that eventually made its way to the sea. We brought along one of the smaller boats. I would be the one in the water, and the two younger men would make their way through the miles of weeds that dotted the shoreline. If he was spotted by the shoreline group I could paddle in for a closer look. All of the groups had bags of dead plant material with them. They would light the material for a smokey signal if the missing man was found.

The day was warmer than usual and I was somewhat taken back by the lack of the usual large number of seabirds. They would travel in packs and swoop down to catch their meals. I remember watching one of these birds on a solo expedition as he dove down over twenty times gathering some food. He would leave and come back so I assumed he was taking fish to some kind of nest. It was a boring day of searching, and we were retaining thoughts of calling the search off in our particular area. We had yelled the man's name until our throat was sore.

I had never lost sight of the men on the shore, and they had yelled to me on a few occasions about turning back. We had observed no signal smoke, and we didn't want to become lost as well. I agreed and was about to come ashore when the men started yelling. I couldn't make out what they were screaming, but it was full of fear and warning. The last thing I remember was a large head and neck coming down on me and my boat. There was more surprise than pain.

The stifling heat finally brought me to, and I found myself in a sea of reeds with the boat on top of me. The terrain was unfamiliar and I struggled to get free from the mud and tall grass. The first thing I noticed was the full moon and the awareness that I was still alive. I struggled to stand up and tried my best to listen to any sounds of the group that I came with. Were they still in the area? Were they still alive? And where was I ?

It took me just a few minutes to realize that I had been out for some time. A patch of red began in the eastern sky, and it took me back to the sun raising ceremonies at Far Point. These ceremonies had long faded from the consciousness of my people, and the Duhare had no such tradition. They did pray to their one and only God one day a week, and tried to explain to me that he was really three Gods in one. They used a three leaf blade of grass to try to explain, but I still didn't get it.

I tried to take account of my situation, and quickly realized my boat had a massive hole in it and would not be serviceable. My bow was gone but a bag tied to the side of the boat was there with some edible shellfish. At least I wouldn't die of hunger. My first mission was to find some fresh water. I scanned the area for any sign of large vegetation such as a tree or large plant. Some of the plants in this area had leaves with juicy amounts of water.

Around these parts were strange plants that the natives called pitcher plants. They would capture and drown insects, and I knew that they held water. My plan was to not drink the water, but to use the plant as a vessel if I could find some fresh water. I didn't know how long I would be here, so I thought of ways to catch water if a sudden storm occurred. Skies in the west were dark, and I had to get ready to catch any rain water. The boat was too damaged to try and use it, but I thought with mud and leaves that I could make it into a vessel that could hold some water.

The pitcher plants were hard to find, but the skies delivered and a sudden downpour gave me enough water in the boat to survive for a few days. My only hope was that a search party would find me before the monster that had destroyed my boat and almost killed me. If a search party was sent out I wanted to make sure that they could find me among the tall grass. I cleared an area around the boat and found some driftwood. A large limb was stuck in the ground and some colorful plant material was stuck to the top. This would not only alert a party to my presence but would also help me as I searched the area for food. The seafood would soon rot, so I needed to find other food sources. One was plant sources and any animals I came across. The Duhare made a snake soup, but I stayed clear of them and the leathery pointy nose critter. These demons could be as long as a man. Of course I aso was on the lookout for the monster that had wrecked my boat and almost killed me.

The days were spent looking for food and marking the days on my boat. I put notches in the side of the wrecked boat to indicate the number of days marooned. The nights were cold as I had no source of fire. Plants and part of the boat served as a temporary shelter. Sleep was hard to come by so I watched the night sky. The myriad of stars and a few shooting stars kept me somewhat entertained.

One night I heard sounds like the crying of a young child. From my experience in The Enchanted Valley I had learned that these were the sounds of the small wildcat. They themselves were not a food source but if I was lucky they might have brought in a deer carcass close to my camp. The next day my guessing turned out to be correct. I found the remains of a deer near a grove of trees. It was close to my camp and I was able to drag it to camp. Luckily it didn't make me sick, and I was able to survive a few more days.

Days turned into entire moon cycles. Search parties had not appeared, but the monster had also stayed away. I was thinking one or the other would happen, and I was hoping for the former. The day was cloudy and I was just standing near the watrer, hoping for a canoe or two. The water was clear and I noticed some movement. Scared at first I stood back to take a look. It was not a snake, or the heavy leather looking critters. This one was huge, but not the monster that marooned me here. It had no long snake like neck, but it was as long as two men. It moved slowly and was ding on all kinds of plants. It was not the monster.

This day was not over. I had my head near my boat and dozed off for a nap. Not sure what woke me up. It might have been the snorting and blowing sound coming from the water. I rolled over to my knees, and came face to face with the serpent. I saw the jaws open, and also .I saw the expression of pain and surprise on its face. Also apparent was the spear that had went through its neck. Standing on the shore close to my boat was Shona.

The beast fell on me and the shell of my boat. I rolled to the side and the monster rolled over me and back into the river. The shock soon subsided and I came to my knees with a mouthful of mud and blood. Shona yelled and I did my best to respond as I spit and coughed out what I could. She beached her boat and ran to help pull me out of the mud. We made sure the beast was gone and collapsed in each others arms. A few tears mutated into laughter as Shona realized what I looked like. Mud and blood and reeds in my ears must have been a comical sight. She cleaned me up and then we started asking each other questions.

"I cant believe you found. How could I have been so lucky?"

"Your survival skills are still there Ahki. The bright flower attached to the large pirce of wood was easy to find. Are you ok?"

"I'm fine, but what about the others?"

Shona went on to tell a tale of days of looking. The man that was with me was sure that I was killed by the beast. Without a body Shona was not about to give up looking for at least a body. Her people believed in proper burials if possible. Village leaders had discouraged her return, but with a crude map drawn by one of the expedition members, she was able to use a small boat to navigate the day or two voyage.

"I was not about to give up on you, although I admit I was a day or two from giving up."

"My only hope was that a search party would at least make an attempt. The reports of my probable death and no doubt the ferocity of the monster discouraged any party. We now need to make sure we return quickly and safely to the village."

Thank goodness Shona brought some food and fresh water. The brackish salt like water I had been drinking for days was keeping me alive but that was avout it. She also brought some bread zand some of the cheese that her people were famous for. In her medicine bag was some of the spiked leaf plant and it had effective pain killing properties. I cleaned up the best I could and we prepared for our trip north. If we encountered no bad weather we should make it back to our village in a few days.

I had some knowledge that I was afraid to impart to Shona. When she had apparently slain the beast, I was struck by one thing. The creature that she had killed was not as big as the one that had first attacked me. My only guess was that this was either a female or an infant of a much larger creature. With this in mind I spent the time on the current river scanning the banks for a creature sunning itself or the water for any fins or humps. A few of the larger critters were spotted in the clear water, but they lacked the hump and large neck of the monster.

Our plan was to make it out of this area as quickly as possible. We had no idea how far the creature traveled, but my guess was that she stayed somewhat close to the sea. This would provide her with a large variety of fish as far as size and numbers. To move quicker we took turns paddling and wanted to get out of the area before dark. Up ahead I noticed a place that seemed to be a good place to camp. We were almost to shore when she hit. She raised our boat out of the water and for a short instance we seemed to be flying like a bird.

We don't know how we survived, but it seemed that the monster thought the boat itself was a creature that had killed its child. She spun us around with such force that we both went fling out of the boat into the tall reeds. I think they hid us from her sight as she was spending all her time smashing the boat to pieces. If we survived today we would need to find our was back to Duhare on foot. The swamp held more dangers than the water. Snakes and quicksand were common in this area. The tide was also unpredictable and we couldn't find ourselves sleeping or resting during a tide surge. The of course there was also the danger of being trapped by one of the monster storms.

After what seemed like forever we could no longer catch sight of the green scaley critter. Maybe she thought that she had killed us. Anyway we hunkererd down in the tall grass until everything on the water was deadly quiet. We cautiously crept to a group of mangrove trees and after making sure that there were no snakes we decided to take turns resting. Moving at night was too dangerous so our plan was to keep moving every day until we found a safe resting place for the night. Our direction was always toward the rising sun.

One of our biggest problems surrounded the tides themselves. We knew that we would need to cross at least one large river, but without a boat that would be suicide. Our only hope would be to navigate the tidal basins and at least make it to the other side of that large river. That particular river was close enough to Duhare that hopefully a camp of a day or two would mean that fisherman would be close, and we could get a boatride with them.

To get to the river we needed to walk along the shoreline for sometime. The sand was deep in some places so we stuck to the area near the dunes. We were tired of seafood and Shona reminded me that they used the plants that grew on the dunes to feed their livestock. She said that some of her people would grind the seeds and mix them with water to make what they called gruel. It wasn't tasty at all, yet the raw fish and shellfish that we were eating was making us both ill.

The next few days were spent looking for a camp. where we could catch sight of any fishermen coming down the river. Before we turned up the river I saw something that reminded me of home. We had experienced the terrible windstorms in The Enchanted Valley more than once. This one looked like the ones up north yet there was little sound. Shona said her people called them waterspouts and down here they for the most part stayed in the water and were not dangerous. It was quite a sight to see.

Our camp was just behind a barrier dune and we had command of most of the area. I spent one entire day looking for driftwood for a three sided structure. The wind from the sea kept most of the rain away yet we needed shelter from the chances of a quick downpour or a little sandstorm. These little sandstorms could temporarily blind a person and we needed a place for protection. The sand could really sting your skin.

On the night before our rescue an event occurred that I considered a good omen. It scared Shona because it involved the star people. I had not observed anything like it and have not since, but it was the most magnificent thing that I have ever seen. The Pathway of Departed Soul was easy to see down here and I explained to Shona how our people believed that this road in the sky was made of souls. The event happened in the middle of the night when I awoke to relieve myself. When I saw it over my shoulder I quickly woke up Shona. We both gasped as it moved out toward the sea. There were three dots of light and it the middle of them was total blackness as the stars disappeared. It moved slowly above us with no sound and as it reached the sea it quickly sped up and disappeared from our line of sight.

The next few days were uneventful. We were too weak toswim the river that basically separated the land of the Duhare from the other clan. It had been weeks so we knew that our people had given us up for dead. We had resolved that we wuld probably die here, but at least it would be in each others arms. Our likes and dislikes were so common that we seemed an easy match. Every night I pointed out to Shona that we soon might join The Pathway of Departed Souls in the sky.

Our last day by the river began with a glorious sunrise. I told Shona that like the star people this was another good omen. We were first alerted by shouting on the river that was unfamiliar to me. She recognized the language of a people that traded with the Duhare. They especially liked the cheese that our people produced. We had no fire or bow to signal with so we resorted to shouts from Shona in the fisherman's language, and me hurling stones in the air that I hoped they would notice.

Finally one of the fisherman turned our way and yelled back at Shona. It was a small boat so they couldn't transport us to the other side together, but our hope was that they would take us over one at a time. The excitement and the grueling trip must have been too much for Shona as she collapsed as soon as the boat reached our shore. We splashed water on her face to bring her back around, but it was obvious that our journey home had another complication. She did manage to explain to our rescuers our plight and who we were.

I told Shona to ask the fisherman if they would help us get back to the Duhare. She told them that if they did that they would be rewarded. I then asked her if they would help me make a kind of carrier for her. My hope was that she would gain her strength, but now the summer heat was making it difficult for her to walk. We made a makeshift carrier out of driftwood and reeds and the fishermen began their transport of us to the other side. The current was swift, and if not for the knowledge of the fishermen we may have drifted out to sea.

Once we made the other side, I tlked to Shona and made sure she was up to the journey. We both were somewhat swollen from the sun and various critters that we had encountered. Sand bugs were common, but we both had been bitten by the floating stinger fish. They didn't look like fish, but their tentacles were somewhat poisonous. She said that her body ached, and the fisherman applied some river mud to our various burns and stings.

The next few days were hot and miserable as we made our way up the coast. Fishing was plentiful, and the constant sea breezes kept us somewhat comfortable. We began seeing dunes and areas that looked familiar. The Duhare were actually on an island surrounded by what they called a moat. To mark their territory that had placed a few flags and pennants on the outer edges of their land.

Shona insisted that she could walk so we dropped the homemade carrier and proceeded on foot. The first territory marker was a banner that we were familiar with. It was an ancient Duhare musical instrument. From here we could make our was home. The fisherman insisted on leaving, even though we had promised a reward for our safe return. We told them that if they ever needed help to mention our names so we could return the favor.

Our first greeter was one of the large camp dogs. I think they called them wolfhounds. To our good fortune a young dog trainer was present. An unfriendly dog of this size would have torn us apart. The dogs barking and the young man's screaming led to a flurry of activity on the island. We crossed the moat and wooden bridge to the shouts and hugs of what seemed to be the entire clan.

CHAPTER 11
CELEBRATION

Runners were dispatched through the village with the news of our arrival. The first responders were elders with medical knowledge to attend to both Shona and myself. My wounds were mostly burns from the sun and tattered and torn feet. The wounds I obtained with the monster were superficial and I didn't need the attention that Shona did. Our hut was still empty although some were getiing ready to move into our empty shelter. The Duhare considered us as dead, although Shona had not been gone that long so they were hoping for at least her return. Seamus had sent some runners to our hut and asked if we could come to the main lodge. I told them that I would be there but Shona was still recovering from her wounds.

I asked one of Shona's friends if she would sit with her while I made my way to the lodge of

Seamus. She said she would and I promised I would not be long. The runners had mentioned to me that Seamus wanted to hear the story and that he had some news for me as well. As I entered the lodge news had traveled fast and this was the most people that I had ever seen gathered in this building.

Seamus gave me a bear hug and offered me drink and smoke. Deer meat was also passed around and that was a welcome sight to me. Shellfish and regular fish were the primary foodstuff for me the past few weeks. Seamus then asked me what happened and he filled me in on Duhare news: "We were surprised and overcome with joy when we heard of your return. How did you survive the encounter with the sea monster?"

"The monster and Mother Nature both tried to do us in. If it wasn't for Shona I would have not made it back. We both were helped by fisherman from another tribe. Without their help we would have perished."

"We all thought you had perished and that Shona's voyage was foolhearty. One of the

reasons was that two of your party never made it back and we weren't sure what happened to them. With that in mind I stopped all expeditions to the southern regions. Shona of course disobeyed the order, but I'm sure you're glad she did. By the way how is she?"

"She'll need some rest, but I m sure she will be back on her feet in a few days."

"Good. We will plan a celebration after she gets back on her feet. Im afraid that I need to impart to you some bad news as well. You had told us stories of raiders from the north. I'm sure they didn't, but it almost seems that they followed you here. A week or so after you left the wolfhounds alerted us to some intruders on the bridge.

When we got to them one wolfhound was dead, but the other was chewing on an invader. Kolman was one of the first on the bridge and he took a spear through the mid section. We were able to drive then off but Kolman succumbed to his wounds a few days later."

I thanked Seamus and took the long sorrowful walk back to the hut. The old custom of the Duhare was to bury in the ground, but digging on the island only resulted in a pit full of water. Seamus had said his body was buried in the swamp. I held off telling Shona about Kolman. They were close friends and in her physical state I didn't think she needed any more worry. It was a long night of grieving.

It wasn't long before Shona was back on her feet. She got back to both her herbal abd food gardening. We enjoyed working the land together. The smaller hut next to our larger one was full of the herbs and foodstuffs that we shared with the colony. They in turn provided us with occasional deer meat and the cheese that the Duhare were famous for.

On one of their visits a Duhare elder informed me that they were going to arrange a celebration for the two of us. It would of course be held in the main lodge with plenty of food and the drinking favorite of the Duhare, wine. It was precious because of how far they had to travel to get the grapes for the intoxicating drink. Not as powerful as the black drink of the north, but it tasted better and didn't make you sick.

The day of the celebration had arrived and we made our way to the main lodge where Seamus had prepared a feast of gigantic proportions. Most of my previous visits were brief, and I hadn't had time to appreciate the magificance of the building. It was not only large, but was decorated with beautiful knotwork. Tables were arranged along the walls. Hooks were placed at intervals so warriors could hang their shield and weapons. In the middle was a large fire pit and spit where a wild hog was being roasted. People would take turns approaching the pit where they would cut off their own slice of meat.

They normally wouldn't drink so much wine, but they were celebrating our return and the wine kept flowing all night. I wasn't used to this drink and I begged Seamus to let Shona and I return to our hut. Before we left I remembered him talking to me about something that he and the elders wanted to remind Shona about. I was unfamiliar with all their customs, and he wanted me to remind Shona about their marriage customs. If Shona so desired the elders felt it proper that since we were living together that we be united in their traditional wedding ceremony. I remember the last thing we discussed before the wine finally got control of us was that is was somewhat funny for people our age to think about the traditional Duhare wedding. We laughed and then fell into the haze of drunken dreams.

The next few days were uneveventful until I received an unexpected visit from Seamus. He requested that we go somewhere private as what he was about to tell me could cause alarm among the colony.

"Ahki tell me more about the raiders from the North. The ones thast you have described in your stories seem very similar to reports that I am getting from our scouts. If they contain Northern tribes like the

Algonquin and Alleghi I fear that our situation here could be in peril."

I told him that the Algonquin spoke our language and had been moving into territory that my people ahd occupied. Their practices were simiar, yet we had noticed that because of the Algonquin many of our people had stopped building mounds and were simply putting the dead on platforms where scavenger birds could do their work. The Alleghi were the ones that I feared and some were led by the giants of the north that we had encountered.

CHAPTER 12
RAIDERS ATTACK

The news of possible raider attacks was disturbing yet not that alarming. The Duhare had the safest village I had ever been in. Not only did they have the normal palisades, but their island home had just one way in and one way out. This made retreat impossible, but was a challenge for any enemy as the one and only bridge could be raised and lowered rapidly. The presense of their large guard dogs would also dissuade the enemy and alert us to their presence.

The good news is that we were confident that if they were to attack that we would be prepared to repel any assault. Shona and I were deeply involved in defense preparation. I had instructed a few of the younger warriors how to use the few bows that we had developed. Their prowess was improving through practice and I spent time locating spots on the swampy island where shooting platforms should be built. We put one on each side of the bridge and others in selected places on the perimeter. Shona was busy preparing poldices and clearing out an area in our herb hut so beds could be placed around the interior.

The entire village was organized into efficient groups that had a specific purpose. One group was in charge of collecting foodstuffs in case of a siege. Water jugs were filled in case our only well was poisoned or made useless by raider sabotage. A few huts were hidden in such a way that any raiders entering the compound would find hard to find. These were to be the places where the smaller children would be hid.

My fear was that all this preparation would die down and we would end up in a state of complacency. Our palisade platforms were finished and supplies in case of a siege were in place. The next few weeks were underscored by frequent bouts of bad weather and little news from scouts that we were sending out into the surrounding countryside. That all changed when one scout breathlessly stumbled into our compound. He had discovered a group of what he described as raiders only a days march from our village. This heightened awareness might have been what saved us.

I told Shona of the raider news. The best place for her would be with the smaller children. I spent a little time showing her how to use a small spear. Many of the Duhare women were trained as warriors, but Shona had always been interested in her plan and herb garden. She stepped up her preparations for treating the wounded. I told her that if fighting occurred I would try to make my way back to help protect the children.

The next few days were rainy and our hope was that the raiders had moved on. That hope was shattered by one of our daily patriols that we had issued since discovery of the raiders. They had discovered a group making ladders that would be used for scaling our palisades. It looked like they had just started so we had some time to prepare in earnest for the attack. I walked Shona to the childrens hut and gave her a final hug before I met with the warriors and Seamus.

Seamus gave the group these final instructions:

"We have lived here in peace for many years, yet knew that the other tribes had occasional disagreements. This looks like the days of legend. Let us fight with the spirit of Cuhullin. We fight for the men and women and children of the Duhare. Consecrate my sword and strengthen the arm that yields it. Purify my mind and secure my heart that the blood it circulates remains pure. Cleanse my soul from doubt. Make fear a stranger and make sacrifice my strong companion. Render me a willing implement of justice. Give me strength beyond my strength. Bless me as you send my soul to battle."

Seamus had just finished his speech or what he called a prayer when the hounds began to howl. We all sprinted to our places along the island and palisades. From my platform I could see the main bridge and gate to our island The dogs were running toward the mainland and I knew raiders would soon be attempting to enter the island. One of the largest Duhare warriors ran to the middle of the bridge. He was completely naked except for his sword and shield. He dodged a few raider spears then was approached by a swarm of raiders attempting to cross the bridge. He killed and wounded all of them until until one swam under the bridge and speared him through the slats.

Other Duhare warriors appeared on the bridge and drug the body of the bridge warrior onto the island.

Raiders now seemed to concentrate their attacks on other parts of the island. Some tried swimming to the palisades yet their progress was halted by the critters in the moat. They were the big lizard type animals that would attack humans. They reminded me of the monster that ny brother and I encountered in the Deer River.

The ladder builders had also built rafts and with long poles were working their way to the palisades. Some were stopped by an arrow or spear thrown from the platforms. A few managed to place their ladders on the wall. The Duhare had large spears they called pikes and they used them to stab and pull raiders off from their ladders. Another large Duhare moverd from platform to platform. He swung a large pole that had some rope like material and a hard spiked ball on the end. Any raider who was unfortunate enough to get on a top rung of the ladder found his brains splattered by the swinging ball.

I was positioned on a platform by myself. A few Duhare ran along the inside of the palisades looking for ladders or raiders trying to scale by themselves. The raiders were now trying to pick of those on platforms by moving rafts within spear throwing distance. As I was loading an arrow in my bow one struck me near the shoulder and knocked me off the platform. The point missed me but the fall almost broke my back. My quiver full of arrows had fallen in the moat. To my surprise Shona helped me back onto the platform. I scolded her for leaving her post but was thankful as she returned to my hut for more arrows. The fight was slowing down and as Shona handed me and arrow I was able to put an arrow through the neck of a spear thrower.

The entire attack lasted but a short time. A blast from a conch shell meant that the raiders were done for now. There weren't any bodies to retrieve as the creatures in the moat to care of the remains.

Shona was still handing me arrows as the siege ended. There were no shouts of victory from our side. The Duhare had always lived in secrecy and safety. Now that they had been discovered the elders feared attacks would continue. Before the last spear was thrown the talk about moving had already begun.

The next few days were consumed with us taking care of the wounded and retelling stories of bravery. Amazingly our only death was the warrior on the bridge and his body was never found. Shona and I used poldices and ointments that we had made to treat the wounded. Our fear was that the wounded would contract a fever and die. Most had wounds to their legs and lower body. Duhare shields were huge and were able to defelect the small throwing spears. We were exhausted after a few days and then began talking about our future.

Chapter 13

Changes

The next few days were spent in deep reflection about our future. Shona and I depended upon the Duhare for many things, yet the promise of more attacks by raiders and other groups led us to discuss our own situation. We appreciated the Duhare cattle and cheese they produced, but we could survive by ourselves by depending on seafood and wild game. The fact that we knew about edible plants and farming meant that we could survive on our own. Other Duhare had left the clan, yet most were afraid to venture beyond the confines of the island.

Shona was still into the clan life and suggested that we speak with clan leader Seamus. He was in the the grand hut on a small couch and was recovering from a stone thrown by the raiders. They had used slings to toss these projectiles over our palisades and one had struck him in the shoulder. He was in in good spirits however and joked about him forgetting to take his shield to battle. He thanked us for our service and then asked us the purpose of our visit:

"Thank you Seamus for letting me an outsider be part of your clan. Shona and I wanted you to be the first to know that we planned to leave the island and to finish our days away from the village. We cant contribute like we did when we were young, and we don't want to be a burden to you and the rest of the clan."

"You both are certainly welcome to stay, but I can appreciate your wanting to finish your days in peace and solitude. Others have done the same as our numbers and birthrates have declined, mostly to disease but if warfare continues I'm not sure how long we can maintain the island. Another monster storm could be the end of us here. We all may need to move farther inland for protection. Pleas take with you any food or building supplies that you may need. As a token take one of our domesticated deer. May God be with you and if we stay please return for a visit.

I thanked him for his kind gesture and was surprised that he gave us one of their animals. They weren't deer as we knew them up north and they provided milk and meat. The one he gave us was pregnant so we were hopefully guaranteed to have a few animals for at least their milk. It was bittersweet to think we were leaving, but we both agreed it was for the best. Our thought now was where were we going and how would we survive without the help of the clan.

We had in our mind some locations that were that close enough to the great sea for a day trio yet far enough away to protect us from storms. One of the first thhings we did was to cllect enough herbs that we could carry in a small wicker basket. They included plants like yarrow which was good for fever and problems of the teeth. We also use it in a polstice for cuts. Wild lettuce was one of our more popular herbs because of its pain killing properties.

Before we left I told Shona that I would make one last visit to the hut of my old friend Seamus. I had not spoken with him since our return from the Altamaha. He had been ill for some time and currently was confined to the bed on the side of his hut. It was only by the grace of the clan that he was able to survive. It took me awhile to roust him from a deep sleep. At first he didn't seem to know me. He sat up in his bed and we began our last conversation:

"Ahki what brings you to visit an old man?"

"No younger than you my good friend. The Gods have just been a little slower in starting my demise. I wanted to tell you that Shona and I have decided to leave the island. Our location is known by many and we fear another raider intrusion will result in a destruction of the clan."

"I have spoken to a few who think the same thing. My time here is short so moving is out of the question. I pray my trip to the other world occurs while I sleep."

"I've left some herbs for your pain and to help you sleep. We may come back after we find a place to see you one more time."

I left Seamus with this prayer that Shona had taught me:

May the Sun bring you energy

May the Moon watch over you at night

May the Rain wash away your Pain

May the Breeze bring you Strength

Shona made her farewells and promised to return to the village after we had established a safe residence. We didn't have many possessions, yet we needed to use one of the gifts that the Duhare had given us, one of the large bridge guard dogs. He was big enough to pull a small sled that held items we might need for our new house. Shona had tools that we had used to cut plants with, but which could also be used to build an adequate shelter. We wanted one close enough to fresh water, but also close enough to the salty sea to give us the breeze to keep away pesky insects. As far as monster storms we would just need to keep a vigilant watch.

We decided to find a location that was within a days walk of the island. Living alone would have its benefits, yet we wanted to be close enough to ask for help if we needed it. I also wanted to be able to warn the Duhare in case another raiding headed their way. Luckily we spotted a mound like hill area near a small stream. What looked to be a large white oak tree anchored the spot. The nuts from these trees were quite tasty. We removed our supplies from the sled and let our camp dog free to roam. This was the lat time we ever saw him.

The next few days were as peaceful and content as days could be. Shona and I weren't in great health and we needed occasional rest, yet time is what we had and we put it to good use. I used some of Shona's hard tools to make a foundation to support a structure against wind and rain. It basically was supported by posts, with a raised floor, a thatched roof with open sides that could be reinforced with moveable walls. The raised floor protected us from snakes and other vermin.

It was now easier to make trips to the great sea. Shona and I would spend half the day collecting herbs and making sure our dwelling was safe for habitation. I would spend some early mornings hunting smaller game like rabbit and squirrel. Shona would look for shellfish, especially the ones with pincers. The ones with softer shells were tastier. She would make a stew with some of our catches. I had a large supply of salt that helped preserve meat for a few days. It would take some time , but I also planned to make a smoking platform to keep items eatable for a few days

Our favorite fish was the red colored one that we could spear in the shallow waters of the estuary. It had a taste sweeter than most fish and it wasn't as bony as some. We also enjoyed crabs and other shelled critters that lived in the sand on the Great Sea or on the smaller islands in the estuaries. Shonas knowledge of plants helped us supplement our diet. Deer stayed more inland and with my weak physical state I wasn't sure I could pull a bow back far enough to kill anything.

Shona seemed to be in better health than me, yet our time here could only be described as paradise. The temperatures were not their normal high because of the cloudy skies, yet they weren't as bad as what I left up north where we were having summer snow. It was not the season for the monster storm and we were confident that our location would be free of any flooding that cost most of the death during these storms. The wind was always a different matter and if theyt happened we would just havee to ride them out.

We had no ventured back to the island city but on occasion had encountered a few fisherman on the beach. They said people like us were leaving the city, yet no raiders had been spotted, and the citizens were in good spirits. We told them to send someone out to let us know how things were going. We went many moons with no contact until the day that the tall stranger came walking across the field yelling my name.At first I thought it to be a messenger from the island village, but as he got closer I recognized the voice. It was my son Onik.

"Father is that you? The people from the village said you were living in this area."

"Onik this is Shona. We let the village a few moons ago and have decided to stay here rather than in the village. We survived one raider attack, but their numbers seem to be getting larger and ours seem to be getting smaller. I can't believe you're here, and I'm sure you have a story to tell."

"I had been living by the Great River with my wife and small child. The summer snow only grew worse and my wife and child died of the lung disease. I buried them where the Deer River and Great River come together. My journey has been long and dangerous, yet with its beauty I know why you. chose to come here."

"Let us prepare you some food, and I'm sure these stories will continue through the night."

The stories continued for days. Onik had not stopped at Fort Mountain because of all the stories of the scary moon-eyed people. He used the rivers as we did, and even had a crude map drawn by the fisherman at a place they called Muscle Shoals. The next few days were spent preparing him a hut for his use. He wanted to return to the village. I told him to be careful and he said using my name got him safe passage. We made sure the hut was big enough. He asked why I was making it so big. I winked at Shona, and told him that the Duhare women are very seductive. A visit to the village might increase this families numbers from three to four.

My life had come full circle. Shona and I would pass our days with beautiful sunrises and sunsets. Onik would thrive in the village and we would see our children during festivals and surprise visits.

This I tell you with no regrets.

-END-